Dear Parent:
Your child's love of read

Every child learns to read in a different way and at his or her own speed. Some go back and forth between reading levels and read favorite books again and again. Others read through each level in order. You can help your young reader improve and become more confident by encouraging his or her own interests and abilities. From books your child reads with you to the first books he or she reads alone, there are I Can Read Books for every stage of reading:

SHARED READING
Basic language, word repetition, and whimsical illustrations, ideal for sharing with your emergent reader

BEGINNING READING
Short sentences, familiar words, and simple concepts for children eager to read on their own

READING WITH HELP
Engaging stories, longer sentences, and language play for developing readers

READING ALONE
Complex plots, challenging vocabulary, and high-interest topics for the independent reader

I Can Read Books have introduced children to the joy of reading since 1957. Featuring award-winning authors and illustrators and a fabulous cast of beloved characters, I Can Read Books set the standard for beginning readers.

A lifetime of discovery begins with the magical words "I Can Read!"

Visit www.icanread.com for information
on enriching your child's reading experience.

For Bill, who loves the
garden!
—A.S.C.

I Can Read® and I Can Read Book® are trademarks of HarperCollins Publishers.
Biscuit and Friends Visit the Community Garden
Text copyright © 2022 by Alyssa Satin Capucilli. Illustrations copyright © 2022 by Pat Schories.
All rights reserved. Printed in the United States of America.
No part of this book may be used or reproduced in any manner whatsoever without written permission except in the case of brief quotations embodied in critical articles and reviews. For information address HarperCollins Children's Books, a division of HarperCollins Publishers, 195 Broadway, New York, NY 10007.
www.icanread.com

Library of Congress Control Number: 2021943589
ISBN 978-0-06-291001-1 (trade bdg.)—ISBN 978-0-06-291000-4 (pbk.)

Book design by Chrisila Maida
22 23 24   CWM   10 9 8 7 6 5 4 3 2   ❖   First Edition

Biscuit
and Friends
VISIT THE COMMUNITY GARDEN

story by ALYSSA SATIN CAPUCILLI
pictures by ROSE MARY BERLIN
in the style of PAT SCHORIES

HARPER
An Imprint of HarperCollinsPublishers

Seeds—check!

Shovel—check!

Watering can—check!

"We're going to the community garden,
Biscuit."

Woof, woof!

Biscuit was ready to explore

as soon as they arrived!

"Stay with me, Biscuit,"
said the little girl.
"The community garden is a big
and busy place."

Biscuit saw rows and rows of plants.

He saw people digging!

Woof!

Could Biscuit dig, too?

"No digging yet, Biscuit,"

said the little girl.

"First, let's find our friends."

Just then, Biscuit heard

a familiar sound.

Bow wow! Bow wow!

Who could that be?

"You found our friends, Biscuit,"
said the little girl.
"Now we can all help in the garden."
Everyone found a shovel or a rake.

Puddles found a worm wiggling

in the soil.

Biscuit found a tiny bird.

Woof, woof!

Did the bird want to play?

Biscuit chased the tiny bird.

Biscuit jumped and jumped.

He landed with a big thump.

Birdseed flew everywhere!

Woof!

Biscuit hurried back to find his friends.
On the way, he saw a woman busy
tugging.

18

Woof, woof!

Biscuit loved to tug and pull!

"You sure know how to tug!"

she said.

Biscuit continued on his way.

He saw brightly colored flowers.

He saw a sprinkler, too.

Woof, woof!

Biscuit ran and splashed.

He gave a big shake.

The water flew all around!

Woof, woof!

Now Biscuit walked up and down

the garden rows.

Where could his friends be?

Biscuit found chipmunks and squirrels.

22

He even found a lost teddy bear.

Biscuit returned it right away!

Biscuit had just seen a butterfly
when the little girl said,
"There you are, silly puppy!"
Oh, Biscuit. Where have you been?"

But then some gardeners asked,

"Is this your puppy, little girl?"

Woof, woof!

"Your puppy
helped me feed
the birds!"

"He helped me
pull the carrots."

"He helped me
water the plants!"

"Your puppy found my teddy bear.
I hope you'll bring him again."

Woof, woof!

"Funny puppy!

You made lots of friends

and helped in the garden today.

There's still time for digging. . . ."

And time to meet another friend, too!"

Hop, hop!

Woof, woof!